Miss Bindergarten Stays Home from Kindergarten

by **JOSEPH SLATE**

illustrated by **ASHLEY WOLFF**

SCHOLASTIC INC.

New York   Toronto   London   Auckland   Sydney
Mexico City   New Delhi   Hong Kong   Buenos Aires

For Donna Brooks, who never—well, hardly ever—stayed home from kindergarten

J.S.

For Maria and Pumpkin, the real Miss Bindergartens

A.W.

ISBN 0-439-44244-3

Text copyright © 2000 by Joseph Slate.
Illustrations copyright © 2000 by Ashley Wolff. All rights reserved.
Published by Scholastic Inc., 557 Broadway, New York, NY 10012,
by arrangement with Dutton Children's Books, a division of
Penguin Putnam Inc. SCHOLASTIC and associated logos are
trademarks and/or registered trademarks of Scholastic Inc.

12 11 10 9 8 7 6 5 4 3 2 1   2 3 4 5 6 7/0

Printed in the U.S.A.   14

First Scholastic printing, September 2002

On Sunday morning, sad but true,
Miss Bindergarten got the flu.
"I'm aching and shaking right down to the bone.
Tomorrow I fear I shall have to stay home."

On Monday—

Miss Bindergarten stays home

from kindergarten.

But at school—

Adam hangs his jacket.

Brenda stores her doll.

Christopher asks,
"Where is Miss B?
I don't see her at all."

"**G**ood morning, kindergarten. I'm sorry to have to say,
Miss Bindergarten called in sick and won't be here today

"I will be her substitute. My name is Mr. Tusky.
I hope you'll help me through the day—I'm just
a wee bit rusty."

Danny says, "I'll take you round!"

Emily shows off Lizzie.

After lunch, Franny moans, "My tummy hurts. I'm dizzy."

On Tuesday—

Miss Bindergarten *and* Franny

stay home from kindergarten.

But at school—

Gwen fills in the calendar.

Henry names who's who.

Ian cries,

"Without Miss B,

I don't know what I'll do!"

"I know you may be feeling sad,
but there's not a thing to fear.
Miss Bindergarten sent lesson plans.
I have them all right here."

"We'll sing a song, we'll read a book—
oh, here's what we will do.
Franny and Miss Bindergarten
would love a card from you."

Jessie paints a get-well card.

Kiki prints a letter.

enny's card says, "I feel hot, but I hope you're feeling better."

On Wednesday—

Miss Bindergarten, Franny, *and* Lenny

stay home from kindergarten.

But at school—

Matty snacks on crackers.

Noah slurps a sip.

Ophelia shares her celery, carrot sticks, and dip.

Patricia says,

"It's sharing time."

Quentin does a trick.

Raffie's yo-yo twirls and whirls.
"Uh-oh," he says. "I'm sick."

On Thursday—

Miss Bindergarten, Franny, Lenny, *and* Raffie

stay home from kindergarten.

But at school—

Mr. Tusky strums and sings.

Sara drums along. **T**ommy claps and **U**rsula taps to Mr. Tusky's song.

That afternoon—
"It's time to go," says Mr. T. "I hate to say good-bye.
But tomorrow, I'm advised, you'll have a big surprise."

Vicky pulls her parka on.
She's the first in line.

"Mr. Tusky," Wanda says,
"we've had a real nice time."

On Friday—surprise!

Franny, Lenny, Raffie, *and Miss Bindergarten*

are back in kindergarten!

Xavier says, "We missed you!"

Yolanda shouts, "Hooray!"

"Mr. T was fun," says **Z**ach, "but I'm glad you're back today!"

"Thank you, kindergarten. I'm feeling so much better.
I know we're all excited to be once again together.
I never will forget your lovely cards and wishes."

They made me feel that you were near,
blowing get-well kisses.
And I'm oh-so-very proud, as proud as I can be,
that you worked like little troupers for our dear sub, Mr. T."

. . . especially Mr. Tusky.